Voices of Ether

Collection of Poems

Wasef Rana

ISBN: 9798839565999

Cover design by: Ahmod Nusaiba Nawar

The book is dedicated to my parents and brother who took the time and effort to tolerate every vile theology I have gathered to conduct research in order to construct.

Contents

Acknowledgment

My family

My mothers side who cheered me on forward despite my unusual taste in genre.

And my fathers side for exponentially motivating me to pursue the art via rebellion

My faculty members back in LSC(London School of Commerce)

Their relentless support to see me succeed had been a tremendous help and I highly doubt I could ever repay their debt even if I had to sell my soul it still wouldn't cause a ripple in the ocean of labour they had put in me.

To my Two special batch mates

And lifelong friends

From University life in LSC

The foundational psychological support one couldn't live without

I owe this to them.

To the very special one whose continual support ignites my soul to move forward.

List of Names in Initials I would like to add.

The book is dedicated to my family members

my parents

Dr A.R
T.R

R.R

My second mom
Bubuni Khammi

My mamas
SZ
MZ(CFA)
EZ
SBZ

Dr SKD
BBB

Sensei J R (BBA)

My cousin sisters (my supporters)

IM
AN
ATU
FN
FRT
ANT
NR

And also another section

To the Dulabhais

Who taught me more of insight
I thank you all
For always believing in me
I honestly never would've understood the value of human beings until I met them

Men of virtue merit
Men of kindness
Men of honour
In gentle tidings
Men I have the privilege of
Knowing
A true yet instant bliss

RK
ARS
AIH
ZM

MY Cousin Brothers(my roots)

MSZ
RZ
MUZ
OK (Nemesis)

And a list of people without whom I can't cover the book
List of inspirations contributed to my book, my success and future.
Companion and friends:

TSS
KF
SM(TJ)
RS
AA
SKL
SZ
MD
SC
HAT
SJ
MH
AB

Faculties of LSC

ZUR
FR
WZ
WA
S Sir
SU Sir

Members of the anonymous crew for inspiring me towards movement and discipline through fitness.

RMI Bboy Rads
IA Bboy Smile
SA Bboy Amkk
SM Bboy Crazy Phyx
AIO Bboy Olive

Favourite quotes

" finance is the blood of the country" WZ (2017)

" It's not what you do, but how you do it" ZUR (2017)

"I don't fear a man who practises a 1000 techniques for one day

But

I fear a man who practises 1 technique for a 1000 days - Bruce Lee" SJR (2012)

Lastly

To the faculties and the management of the institution I am currently working in, contributed immensely by giving me the time and honour I needed to complete this book. Which wouldn't have been possible without this help for which I am eternally grateful for. Thank you all For being a part of this journey . As you will be In many more books to come.

Special thanks to ANN for publishing this book.

About the Book

The book contains anthologies under three sections

Silent Cries of Broken Codes

Talks about heartbreaks

And romantic poems

Far Cry

Talks about social stigma

Ode of Ether

Talks about the writers dreams and hallucinations

About the Author

Wasef Rana is an MBA graduate, a school teacher and a paranormal enthusiast obsessed with the human emotions and psyche along with the dark heritage of nations aligned.

When he isn't busy writing, he studies ghosts, divinity ,nature and also can be found in the local gyms chasing fitness.

Legend has it.

He comes and goes in different shapes. Yet never satisfied. Maybe someday he will be.

Author

Wasef Rana

Index

Dark Stems

I bleed
Slowly
In silence
As a halo
Of dark stems
Strewn right across
My face

Coveth my eyes
In pain
I wither
In agony
I let out quiet
Muffled screams
To squeamish
For anyone to hear
Yet anyone cares
Hard enough to notice
My torturous
Hell
Honestly
All my secret cries
Fall on deaf ears

People are much like
These stems
They would rather
Believe the lies
Of their own
Conformity
Than stepping
Up to help
Me......

Yes I bleed
A halo of dark stems
Coveth my eyes
Yet in vain
My silent
Yet
Painful cries
Fall in
Deaf ears
People are yet
Too busy
Hearing their delusional
Lies
Than heed my dark
Screams
From the
Very near.....

Wrecked

Prayers
Of the marred

Broken Voices
That violently
Echos

Flowing
Chaotically

From my dilapidated
Walls
Of my gloomy
Brittle Room

Like a thousand
Butterflies
Fluttering
In vehemence
In my little heart

Similarly

Like
Warm water
Flowing out
Of broken
Porcelain

Painted sorrows
Etched To heart
Sketched within the mind
Stretched yonder a point
That content a million tomorrows
As time endlessly flies by
Like fluttering sparrows

Painted lament
Till
I hear the voices
No more

Painted hatred
Till
These cries
Turns
To laughter

Grief
To
Joy

Painted in my own
Little Piece
Of tranquillity.......

Imperial Kings

Hastings of the House
Byron the Bard
Lords of The past
As you all
Have ruled
Valiantly as ever

Honor Had Not Died
With you
As
You Rest within your
Cascaded Coffins
Peacefully

Lord of the Imperials
Ravagers of Nations
Takers of Feeds
That
Fed on dine
Drank this soils wine
Bed under Tattered Tin roof
Of Mothers concubines

Now

Perished
One with the soil
whose sons blood it drank
Now mixed With yours

Yes
In this House
You murder
I cried
Yet History lied
Swiftly
Yet
Quietly

After Your
Untimely Passing

For I
Mournfully Yours
Restlessly Holding back
My Tears

As My
Heart
Beats For You

As Silently
As A mouse.......

Calm

Empty mind
Calming breeze
Silently flows
Through the skies

Trees sings
as flowers dance
They rejoice
Relish the solitude
Of this secular
Desolation

Nature doesn't
hold such folly
their emotions
sever any
Unnecessary
Tethers
As
They
Ascend beyond
Spiritual limits
all the while being still
Despite being bound
Against will
They watch
They Study

They mimic
Quietly

Nature calls
For the void
For it requires
Nothing
To be bound by
No loyalty
Of pact
hence
The thought of
A whistleblower
Never born to exist

Where
no one don't
Have to swear
To
No oath
Nor
Shed no blood
To sign the pledge

Be empty
In time
Become
Wind.........

Nana

What am I about to say are about my memories of nana
I never spoke to him much ....
Many would speculate I may be off my rocker.
Yet I am sure whoever felt it must've felt it.

Nana and I never shared any memories. the only memory I had with him is when I used to watch him stare into the abyss... There were times that I would turn off the TV and watch him stare at the empty vacant walls which had made me much more curious to watch the walls with him rather than the TV.
Yes, a child and an old man staring into the everlasting vacancy that preoccupied the empty lot of space in that house in Dhanmondi during 2006. A little boy on the verge of becoming a teen and an old man on the tip of meeting his maker. Empty is filled by vacancy as life is preoccupied with death.

What was he actually staring at?
I would wonder
Or Who? I would ask
Is it Allah? I questioned
Is it Azrael? I doubt
Or some celestial being that stayed with Nana ever since that

"day"....

I was deeply curious

Imagine a scene where there is a child and an old man sitting in a wheelchair, imparting hallow breaths, inhales and exhales of a ventilator,
Both staring in the eyes of oblivious darkness staring back at them.
An ominous eerie manifestation that looms around him
And strangest thing I felt it....
It's like he knew
He definitely knew
He just won't tell....

Mom claims
That limitless excitement within me
Died down due to her prayers in Hajj.
She couldn't have been more wrong

Nana was the one responsible for extracting that out of my system...
How?
Simply put,
by intriguing my curiosity then dragging it down to a level I was simply afraid to act on it......
Instinctively
Day after day sitting with him spending at least half an hour just watching
The wall
Even at times Nanu thought

Something was odd me
Yet I never expressed what I saw or felt till now. The man beyond normal.... He is one rare being. They say a war hero reminisces the previous battles, relieves those memories even worse, torn by war.

But nana was a survivor

Nana never cheated death
He overcame the scales of balance
He was
The Man who Tipped the scales of Balance to his favor despite all impossible odds
He was one step closer towards meeting Allah ....

He was indeed definition of the indomitable ....

Nana taught me to actually see...
To feel the little things in life....
To question and to always believe in things
most neglect to believe at all....
Yes,
Nana and I never spoke a word to each other....
Nana taught me the true abject meaning of divinity
The tranquillity that resides around us....
We just don't notice.

Despite evolutionary enhancement
We cut corners......
Instead to feel yonder mortal horizon
We confine ourselves

To live rather than the namesake
of living

Simply
God created us free
We created rules
That binds us to what?
Materialism
Quantified by number
Qualified by words
Even tombstones have names too
Doesn't that ever carry a value......

Getting back to nana

I never spoke at all
I simply observed
The manifestation that poured out of him
The faithful glow that is not even human
Surrounded him ......
That's divinity ......

The more I observed
The more I felt my eyes being peeled open
By a benevolent force of nature
A force that sticks to a person
Nana owed a debt.
The debtor stayed with him
Till nana finally paid in full with his last breath
By April 2007 ....
Is this what happens when a person survives death?

Death stays with him
Till that debt is paid.

Yet however
I wish to meet him after death
And just talk to him
And his life
His memories
His childhood
His past life. ....
And later
I want to know that being that kept company of my grandad after he confined himself to a wheelchair....
To those who are wondering the moral of the story...
There is nothing to it
The abyss of mystery
Smiling back
From the empty
hollow depths
Of oblivion.

I feel alone

As my eyes
Reach
It's deep hallows

My soul
That hangs
From the gallows
Within the heart
Hung
By the web of arteries
That surrounds it
As cord

I feel alone
As my collarbones
Begin
To appear
I feel no
Hunger
Just thirst

Yet
My belt shrinks
Like my waist

I feel alone
Empty
Like the wind
Of the void
That acknowledges me
And
The darkness
That beckons my name
"Come hither"
I step closer
"Come hither"
I wilt
I wither
"Come hither"
As I float towards it
Like flames on ether
Till
I feel it's chilly
Yet warm
Embrace
Coiling me
Tightly
Yet with such
Softer care

For the first time
Finally
Someone
acknowledges
Me.......

I perish

Smiling
To that thought
For all the years
I have fought
Finally met its end
From darkness
I was born
To
Darkness
I return......

Martyr

Was it the void that killed him?
No
It was the negligence
that had
slid him into
obscurity

It was negligence
That made him
Invisibly oblivious

It was abstinence
That made him the
oddball
A reek of sin

Yes
It was humanity that murdered him
Humans butchered his faith
And
People just watched
While his soul was fed
To the dogs

Dilapidated
Was his heart
Marred
Was his soul

He wasn't an unsung
Cadaver
rather
His lyrics
Were coptic to others ....

Ambivalence

Thrown into the abyss
with a scattered mind
my astral soul
freely
roams
the breezes
of

these lost winds
as
my limbless heart
Aimlessly floats through
The continuum
Silently heals
With each strides......

She was shy
In the
Month of Beating Hearts
Hiding from my scented letters
As my mind
Madly sought for her
As
my only hope
of sunshine
a cure
For my loneliness

She was smiling
In the
Month of Rain
Eating apples
from the trees
While bathing in the blessed shower
With a distant dream
of sailing around the isles
As she was a dream to others across the land

She was to wed
In the
Month of Clans
To the heart throb from desolate
dreams
Barbwire gripped my arrhythmic heart
Jagged shrapnels scraping my chest...

Dreams

Let the darkness
Sing u
Silent lullabies

Close ur eyes
As
I close mine

I'll see you
As
You see me

In one of our
Own
Lucid dreams.......

Beneath

Beneath these skies
A soul dies
Underneath these stars
There's an alien from Mars

Beneath the black n blue
A heart broken for an unnamed who
Underneath the shadows
Lurks the evil which never bows

Beneath the flaming pyres
Lies the ashes of countless martyrs
Who took a bullet in name of love
Resides down below than above

While that same bullet
Eaten by rust
As their bodies die
flesh devoured by
A carnival of maggots
In time
It's all dust...............

Bird

Bird of the throne
That sits on top
Of man's crown
For
all those
conquests
Valiantly fought
Brutally won

Bird of the crest
That made it's home
in the chest
Humbly rests
For the
dormant pride
Which lies sunken
Deep
Within the heart

Bird of the foliage
Made its abode
Within the gut
For all the spoils
Slowly feeding
Humanity's
Infernal addiction
As it
Progressively

Spikes with age.....

Bird of The song
That sings gleefully
on the occasion
When all that of chaos
has been resolved

When all that
had been left
of Violence
Finally Simmered

It sings
On the aftermath
Of the dead

The song that signals
evil to sleep
Until its yet to be woken
for another day
Leaving the rest of the slaughtered
To be cleaned

Bird of the songs
the anthem of martyrs
Hung from the trees
As their
names
Hangs from the tombstones
Of our minds

yet
Reminding
Evil never rests....

She's a Mystery

*Sips espresso
Writes profusely*

She's a gift

Profoundly!

gasps
She's fatal to her whims

She's got a history

*He shrinks his eyes
Like a shrew
Sips more from his freshly brew*
"Neh"
Doesn't bother much as he continues

Yet she's amazing
Perfect for her flaws

See?

Her deep scars
How bravely
She withstood
With dignity and strength
The wrath of those claws
Meant for disgrace
Yet
she was the last woman standing
A survivor

Yes!

A martyr

No!?

For she has fought with honour
With fire
Still
burning at her core.

*Puts down the pen
Will write
But when?

Sips more
of his warm brew
Crumbles up any ideas that flaw
Back at it
Began to draw*

She may be a total mystery
She does have trust to spare
To lift that huge emotional
Burden
Weighing on her shoulders
Yet her brutality comes from peers

She may fall for her whims
For it's human nature
It's the purest form of integrity
Yet her fatality comes from people

She may have a history
Don't we all
Yet she maintained her composure
Endured the torture
Bore the aftermath of the overture
That humanity hurled against her
Yes
Yet calamity comes from her own fellow humans

She is a gift from God
A blessing
A life
A vessel
A friend
A guardian
A saviour
Everything.......

*Puts down the pen
Finishes the espresso brew
Past bedtime
Way past ten
Looks at the screen
Where a million eyes drew
Staring back

If I can accept her.
Can you?*

Echo and Canvas

ECHO always thought
of CANVAS
In fluttering beats
Of her palpitating heart

Been there
for him
At his
desperate times

Canvas was well received
With shoulders for support

Butterfly kisses
Which finally she gave
Him
A heart
To love
To understand
To share joys and grief
With
In silence

Angels cried
Martyrs sung

In return
She witnessed
Reality

Turn against her
Blamed her
till her mind
betrayed her

Cruel words
Split

Vows be
Broken

Instinctively
ECHO would
Submit
Forgiving by nature
She pretends to cascade
her

Escapades and endeavours
Yet
Still her weeping heart
Throbs
By each rhythmic beat

Mimics mockingly
As her arrhythmic soul
Sobs
As her void of lamentation continues
To devour
Her soul
Her mind
Herself ....

ECHO yearned to be cared
As love caresses
Her
Tender soul

By means of lasting pleasure
For eternity

She always did
Have that
sweet smile
Across
Her lips

Canvas betrays
Pain so

Paradoxically unbearable
Anxiety soon befriends her
Depression soon joins in the club

Her limbless heart
Now

Lost in the abyss

Canvas
Is
No more
Than the vile air
Of sin
He breathes in
Proudly

Even though

ECHO
Her reckless emotions
The ties that bind her
Forces her to smile
Further cascading
Her emotions
As she's lost in her own
Cavernous void
Undisturbed

It was undoubtful
The way ECHO trusted CANVAS

CANVAS slips

As songs turns to symphony

Echos daydreams stirred to gloom
Canvas treachery
Ashes and water covered the room

For now she is the last resort
The lions roar at the
Tip of her doorstep

To feel the prick of needle
Cold and fear
As
The monstrosity forth her
Embrace her

Within her mind
Echo falls
Down to the coldest waters
As it hits her
like
Thousand knives
Thousand ways
Thousand times
Mercilessly
Silence never breaks

Yet she screams internally.

Echo saw love
Within Canvas
Within those restless
Eyes of his
Purity within his sin
Evil was which
She thought was kind

Woe

She didn't survive......

Dearest Society

Dearest Society
When I was born to u
You held me closer
Than I thought you would
Showered me
Pampered me
Taught me things
You liberate me
Because I am a boy

Dearest Society
If I was a girl
Would u have done the same

May be the 1st 10 years
Of compassion
And then comes pain
Emotional
Physical
Yet
Worse
psychological

Dearest society
You eagerly wait
For incoming statuses
For you praise me
Your son
The result of your reputation
Uprising
What abt ur daughter?
Isn't she the one
Responsible
For giving life
After 9 staggering months
Worse
9 painful hours

Dearest Society
Wen I
Your son
Breaker Of Rules
Casanova of Crimes
Invade
Young oaths
With false hopes

And unkept promises
And what do you do
While being my parent
You watch silently
Sidelining my mischief while
Using the Phrase

"boys will be boys"

While my sister
Talks to any
U shame her
With words sharper
Than a samurai blade

Dearest society
As your age and time prospers
So fast
yet u encourage me
To keep up
To be one of em
To become one u c fit

My dearest society
If my sister
were to keep up
You slow her down
Violently
I wonder why?

My dearest society
I have made
mistakes
None of which
In account u take

But if my dear sister
Made an err
U burn her soul
Till mentally she's no more

My dearest society
Together we are one
Entity
Under the moon
The sun
Within an entire
Galaxy
I write this ode to u
to decode elden rules
much needed to be forgotten

My dearest society
Like u torn me
Out of your womb
As the same
Why
U tore the womb
Out of my sister's body

Turning dignity into ashes
The same dress of respect
that presented to queens and angels

It isn't too late
For a change

Be kind to her
As you are to me

And what do I do
I watch

I
Watch in silence
It's quite unfair
Dearest society
Believer of just
Show some mercy
My sister is free
Like me
Pray
Have mercy
Sincerely
Yours
Ur loving son
Man.................

Secret Was He Love Was She

Secret was he
In his web of lies
Conjured from his mouth
In scented breath
Love was she
Accept the deceit
Blindly
With hugs and kisses
Poetry and songs
were
Sung in silence.....

Secret was he
As he spilt
Seeds
More venomous
Than toxic or ivy
Under the Sheets
Love was she
Accepts those seeds
Thinking of them
As flowers
Yet to blossom
As it lay conceived
Slumbering
In her womb

Of Thick
crimson waters.....

Secret was he
He lies as he swore
Where as all this time
Lying from his core
He wasn't alone
As someone was
Locked behind
His closet door

Love was she
As she came crying
Of the truth she conceived
Soon
She is positive
An infant in her womb

Secret was he
Wanted liberty
From the unborn life
As he refuse to father
Love was she
Willing to try
Sought solutions on the tap screen
Almost to cry
She's a mother to be

Secret was he
Screamed bloody murder
Towards the mother
Who wanted the infant
Alive as its peace

LOVE was she
Constantly urging
To give it a try
With a lil might
Her babe can be as
Bright in life
More than they ever be

Secret was he
Failed to realise
The stranger
Managed to unlock
The door
Stumbled
On the floor
So clumsy was she

Love was she
Her heart cracked in parts

Untold

Said nothing
Left the two
In Silent Tears

Soon

Secret was he
Lead a life as he meant to be
With the girl
He locked earlier
Love was she
Now no more
Hangs in the gallows
Behind her own door

Innocent was it
With the babe gone
Destroyed in the very same
Bathroom
it was once discovered
Flushed to it's
Uncalled doom
forever

Love Was She
Beneath Her
Cascaded fears
Lies her love
for a living sin

As

Secret was he
in his bed of lies
Tar Filled chest
He is
breathing sin

Pathological lies
flew freely
Yet He remains
distant from the one
That desires
Him
The most
As he desires many a none
But himself

Oh Fate
be a little less cruel
Will you?

Secret Was he
Which is why
He always lied

Love Was she
Which is why
She found it
Quite Hard
To confide

Until
Finally

Love Was she
How cruelly She hung
As

Hope Left

Cascading
her dreams
Permanently
Ending her pursuit of the escapade

As

Her neck
Comfortably
Embraced
By the noose
Of her own silken seams
Her Faith Quickly Faded
As quickly as
Her breath

Desperate Gasps
As air within her
Escaped Until nothing left
But the slow beats of her heart
Becoming slower
To none

Until the
Living silhouette
Of
Her dangling soul

Hanged gracefully
On its own

Under The Stairs
Under the light
In which she hung
In darkness
Was she
Swallowed........

Secret was he
Beneath his lies
As
Her love

Housed
His sin
Sanctioned the babe
In its unhallowed tomb
To be such deceptive

Yet
Secret Was He
The One
To carry out
The rite of death
Of an innocent
So
Swiftly
Without any mercy
Without any remorse
Deliverance
Of a bitter testament

Yes
Indeed
Love was she
A price to pay
For her in earth
For him afterwards

Love was she
As she hung
Before she died
She heard
Her unborn babe cry
From the bathroom
His infant squeals
The cries of an unborn fetus
Resting in the bathroom sink
As he
Remained the bornless one
While its mother
The heartbroken wrote
A two line song
Morals that matched
No strings attached
SECRET WAS HE
LOVE WAS SHE.............

Failure

I was aware
Of every moment
Of every waking
Living seconds
That slowly passed by

Harsh words
Flew across
The room like
Flying knives

Each corner
Of each harsh letter
Stabbed me
Mercilessly

Of parents
Of relatives
Of friends

Every family
and non
Became foe

Funny thing
They still is

I felt
Every slice
Of every severed nerve
They cut
Out of me

Every tug of flesh
They pulled
By their hook
Crooked my honour
Decapitated my dignity

My mind couldn't
Take much of it

Every flesh
Were pulled from my bones
Until nothing was left
Until absolute darkness
Devoured me
Darkness and pain

Thousand other
Intense emotions
began to
flood in

Agony
Pleasure

Fury
Ecstasy

All blended
Into a single
Piercing noise

Until that very
Darkness
Was broken
By sparks
Of twinkling starlight

The pain
The light
The noise
All merged
Took shape

Of my own prison
I call my home.....

Chasing Butterflies

As I Chase butterflies
within a twisted storm
though my slumber

May linger
Down the fathoms
Of abyssal deep

Visages haunt
My ambivalent mind
Yet
My restless soul
Estranged

My sorrow
My fears
Envisaged by my anxiousness
As my hunger
May
Seem starved to thin
As my cuts and scars
Bleeds my skin......

As I chase butterflies
Within a twisted storm
Sleep separates from me

As my mind filled with racing
With echoes of countless
Thoughts
Followed by
Endless voices brays and calls

While caffeine marries
My blood
Deeply infused
My heart refuses
To beat slowly

As I chase butterflies
Within this twisted
Storm

I see people
Hung from trees
Crimson red
Filling the skies
While the sun and moon
Are watchful eyes
Hovering above
Watching
My every move
Observing
My every Emotions

Shadows never stop humming
Behind my back
Yet escaping in faint glimpses
As I search back for them

Leaving empty traces
For me to follow
And cold cases
For others to see

Judgemental thoughts flies
Like a thousand swallows
flying as one....

As I chase butterflies
Within this twisted storm
I will eventually catch one
At least

And finally
ill relax
Take it easy
Perhaps take a bath

Then sleep........

Empty

Empty graves
Full of null
Full of void
Bleeds decay
Of molten flesh
Food for maggots
Soul severed
From its earthly tethers
Enters the null
Enters the void
Enters the empty
Breathtakingly silent
Even for
A
Breathless soul

Empty bed
Full of thorns
Full of vines
Bleeds dark
Red
Of
broken hearts
Sleepless nights
Restless thoughts
Meaningless fights

Empty desks
On them
Lie empty pages
Lie empty envelopes
Of due paychecks
Of
People yet to receive
For their laboured
Agonising pain

Yet greed
However had other plans

Empty fields
With
Empty seeds
Where nameless
Where countless
Where purposeless
battles were fought
So violently
That crystal
Blue skies
Gave birth
A crimson hue

Blood filled the soul
Iron filled the air
Rage fuelled the heart
Envy and wrath
Fills the goal

Empty hours
Of aimless chase
Empty labour
Against time

No productivity ever
Produced while haste
But
Only serves to
Corrode the servitude
Overtime

Empty beacons
Of hope
Of lies
While people
Mindlessly boggles

Abstained from the lies
They preach
Yet in practice
People abstain from light
Through teaching.

All the while
In the everlasting
Darkness

Do we ponder
While our
Own selves asks why

We don't say
Anything
But smile
We say
It's okay
We lie......

Curtains

Behind the curtains
Of man
Lies the devil

Behind the curtains
Of life
Lies death

Behind the curtains
Of time
Lies oblivion

Behind the curtains
Of love
Lies insight

Behind the curtains
Of darkness
Lies abyss

Behind the curtains
Of the great chase
Lies void

Despite all
We race
We fall
They rise
The take off
Where we left

The cycle repeats

There's no end.....

Paradox

From the black orb
Of dilated pupils
To the egg white
Of the eye

Nadir to zenith
Lies
Just yonder
The split
Of scarlet red
From blood

Silent cries

Of scorched souls
In crimson agony

Turns muffled
Quiet sound of flowing
Life
Through veins and beyond

I
Travel inside
The core
Of
The soul

Where the void of black
Is none but
A
Thick veil

To shroud me
From myself
Only to
Wonder why
I
Wander among
An unfathomable

Paradox
Am I stuck
Or am I not

The endless intense wailing
Can be heard
Within the vacant walls
Of this purged inner
City halls
Where
The deafening roar
Of desolate flames
Roars madly in confusion
As if
nothing burns
It the flames never die
But lively burns
Yet
Nothing evaporates……

www.ingramcontent.com/pod-product-compliance
Lightning Source LLC
LaVergne TN
LVHW040911150826
845672LV00007B/1991

* 9 7 9 8 8 3 9 5 6 5 9 9 9 *